Where Madness Reigns
The art of Gris Grimly

Baby Tattoo Books®
Los Angeles

(on previous page)

High Contrast
ink and watercolor on watercolor paper 2006

ISBN: 978-0-9778949-8-7 Trade Paperback
ISBN: 978-0-9793307-8-0 Limited Edition Signed Hardcover

First Edition

10 9 8 7 6 5 4 3 2 1

Published by Baby Tattoo Books®
Los Angeles
www.babytattoo.com

Design by Laurie Young

Manufactured in China

Rise Gut Tongue Rise
ink and watercolor on watercolor paper 2006

Where Madness Reigns
The art of Gris Grimly

Bop Pills
mixed media on canvas 2007

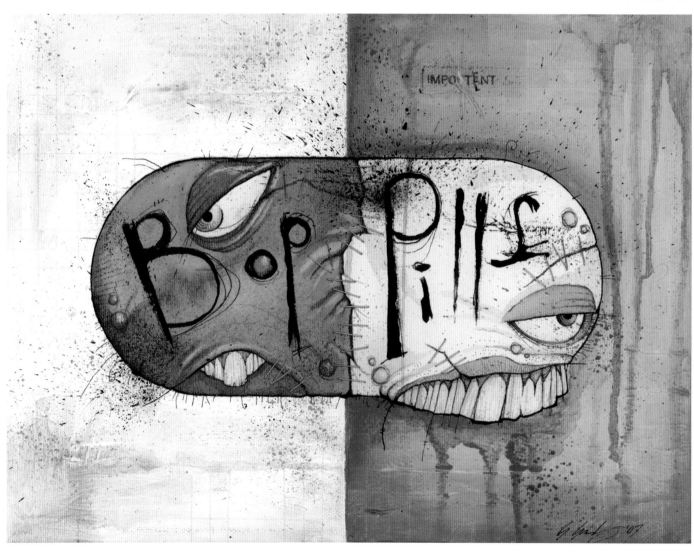

Pill Head
mixed media on board 2007

Pharmaceuticals to the Rescue
mixed media on board 2007

Ride of your Life
mixed media on board 2007

Our Lord the Flayed One
mixed media and collage on board 2002

Don't Worry, your Child's with Me at the Tea Party Doing Coke with Bugs Bunny and Abe Lincoln
mixed media and collage on board 2006

How to Disappear Completely
mixed media and collage on board 2004

WOOD

The Harrowing of Paradise
mixed media and collage on board 2005

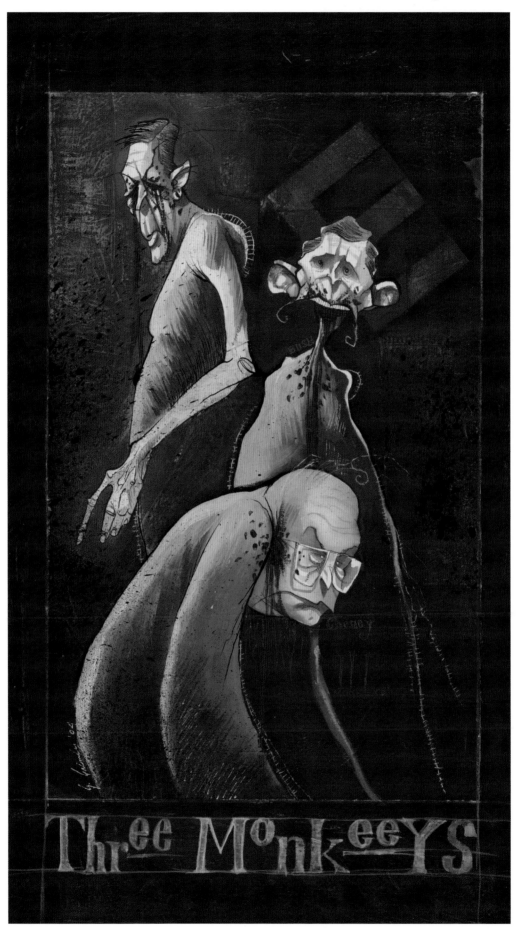

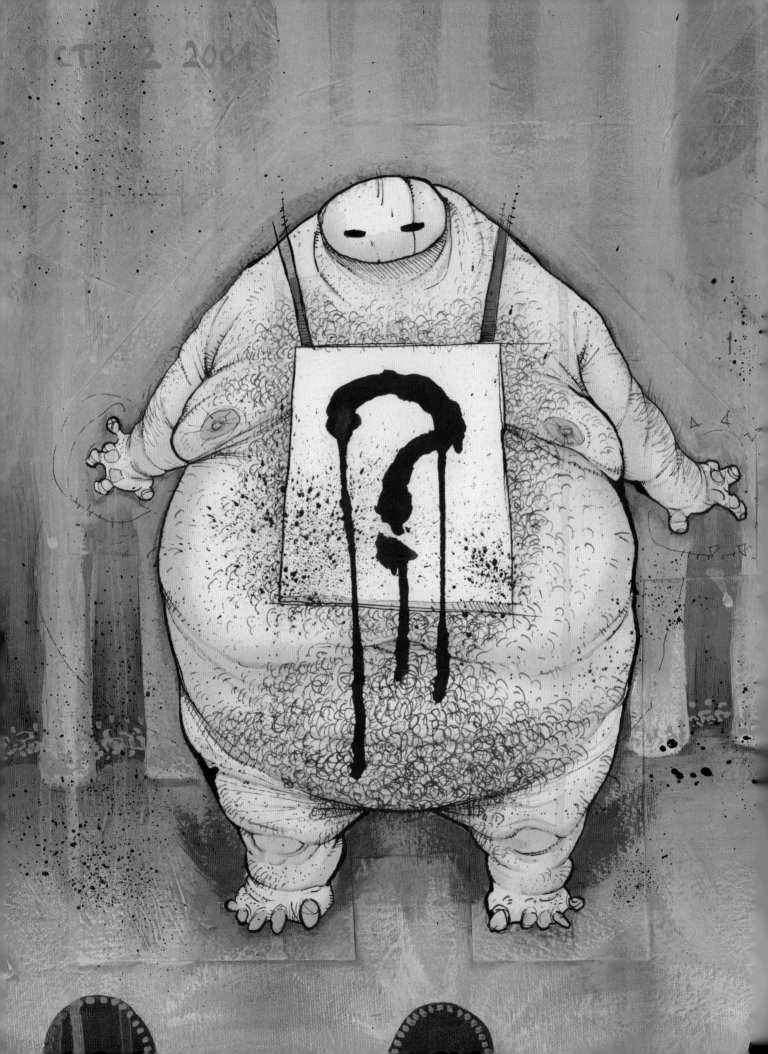

An Ode to the Modern Anomalies

mixed media and collage on canvas 2005

The Thing on the Side of the Road to Nowhere
mixed media and collage on canvas 2006

The Weeping Song
ink and watercolor on watercolor paper 2003

Apart
ink and watercolor on watercolor paper 1999

Alone
ink and watercolor on watercolor paper 1999

The Birth and Death of Everything
white acrylic and ink on gray paper 2005

The Customary Birthday Fish
white acrylic and ink on brown paper 2004

Goddess of the Creeps
white acrylic and ink on gray paper 2002

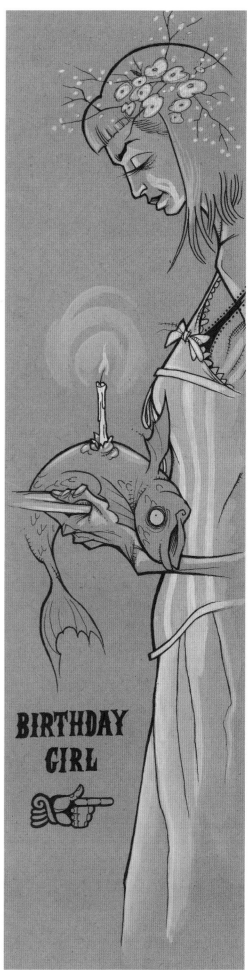

BIRTHDAY
GIRL

To Walk the Night

ink on illustration board 2006

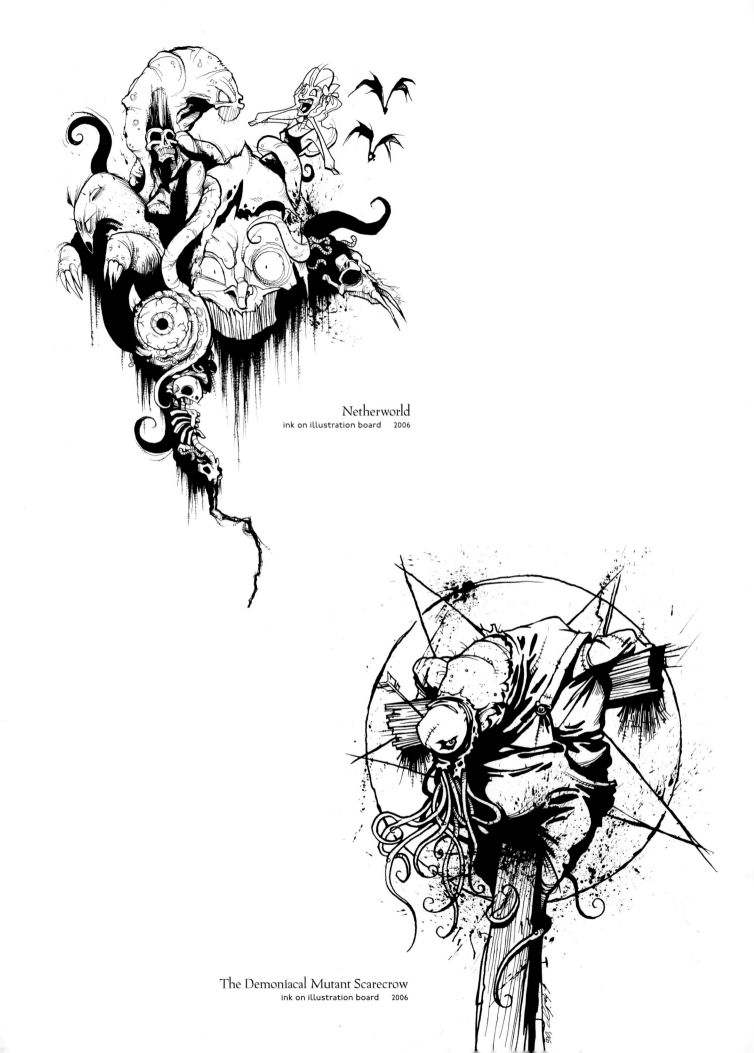

Netherworld
ink on illustration board 2006

The Demoniacal Mutant Scarecrow
ink on illustration board 2006

Ugly Girl in a Pretty Frame
ink on illustration board 2002

Welcome Foolish Mortals
ink on illustration board 2007

G is for Gallows
ink on illustration board 2002

The Unconventional Amour
ink on illustration board 2003

Ghoul School
ink on illustration board 2002

Mayor

ink on illustration board 2001

Private Dicks

ink on illustration board 2001

Frog Legs

ink on illustration board 2001

Fly Guy

ink on illustration board 2001

Natas Pringle

ink on illustration board 2001

Shaman

ink on illustration board 2001

Louie Hooks

ink on illustration board 2001

Finger Fairy

ink on illustration board 2001

Insanity Painted in
Crimson and Nicotine
mixed media and collage on board
2004

The Purging of the Roses
mixed media and collage on board 2003

Sunset Souls for the Taking
mixed media and collage on board 2006

The Adventures on Halloween Island
ink and watercolor on watercolor paper 2006

Lou Lou Escapes the Valley of the Zombies on her Noble Lycanthrope
ink and watercolor on watercolor paper 2006

Lure
ink and watercolor on watercolor paper 2006

The Satanic Coven of Justice
ink and watercolor on watercolor paper 2006

Lycanthrope Abduction
ink and watercolor on watercolor paper 2006

Cannibal Cake
ink and watercolor on watercolor paper 2007

Mortimer: Ashes to Ashes
ink and watercolor on watercolor paper 2007

Grue: Bones to Paste
ink and watercolor on watercolor paper 2007

THE
GENTLEMAN
SNOWMAN

The Snottman Christmas
ink and watercolor on watercolor paper
2003

Walking in a Freaky Wonderland
ink and watercolor on watercolor paper
2004

Christmas Cat
ink and watercolor on watercolor paper 2003

Santa Bat
ink and watercolor on watercolor paper 2006

Red Stains on White Snow
ink and watercolor on watercolor paper 2003

First American Vampire
acrylic on canvas 2007

A Redneck Werewolf in America
acrylic on canvas 2007

Misfortune Strikes on Colonel Sander's Farm

acrylic on canvas 2007

Cat and Mouse
acrylic on canvas 2007

Mindy with Her Pet, Wallmount
acrylic on canvas 2007

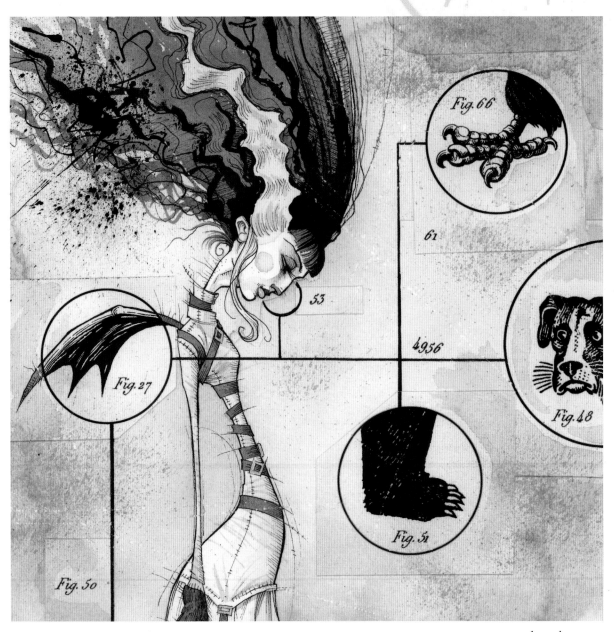

Fig. 66

61

53

4,9,56

Fig. 27

Fig. 48

Fig. 51

Fig. 50

Beauty in the Laboratory
mixed media and collage on board 2007